The Best Single Mom in the World
How I Was Adopted

Written & Illustrated by

Mary Zisk

Albert Whitman & Company

Morton Grove, Illinois

Library of Congress Cataloging-in-Publication Data

Zisk, Mary.

The best single mom in the world : how I was adopted / written and illustrated by Mary Zisk.

p. cm.

Summary: A girl tells how her mother decided to become a single parent and

traveled overseas to adopt her, and describes their happy life as a family.

ISBN 0-8075-0666-4 (hardcover)

[1. Adoption - Fiction.   2. Single-parent families - Fiction.]   I. Title.

PZ7.Z687 Bg 2001 [E] - dc21   00-010208

The illustrations are rendered in gouache on Arches hot-press watercolor paper.

The design is by Scott Piehl.

For more information about Albert Whitman & Company,

visit our web site at www.awhitmanco.com.

For the single best daughter in the world,

Anna Isabella Veronika Zisk.

And for my parents, Mary and Tony Zisk,

who have given me a lifetime of love and support.

My mom

is the best mom in the world.

But she wasn't always my mom.

We love to tell the story of how we

became a family. My mom always begins,

"Before you were born, I lived alone in this house.

"I loved my work and my friends,"
my mom continues.

"But something was missing!" I shout.

My mom hugs me and laughs.
"That's right," she says.

"I wanted to share my happy life

with a child,

a child I could laugh with and learn with.

A child who needed a family."

"Like me!" I add.

"Yes, you!" says my mom. "So I went to an

adoption agency, which helps people find

children who need families.

I wanted to find a child to adopt, to love,

and take care of forever.

"The people at the adoption agency looked high and low,

near and far, all over the world..."

"And found *me*," I cheer.

"Yes, they did. You were born far away across
the ocean and over the mountains,"
explains my mom.

"You were born from the tummy of a
woman called your birth mother.
Your birth mother wanted the best for you,
but she couldn't take care of you.

"She wanted you to have a
family to love you and care for you."
My mom pulls me close.

"So you adopted me!" I smile.

"Yes, I flew across the ocean
and over the mountains
to meet you for the first time,"
says my mom.

"Finally you were in my arms.

You were the most beautiful baby in the world!

I hugged you and kissed you.

I called you my little snuggle bunny and

promised to take care of you forever."

"And home we came!" I always say, finishing the story.

And that's how my mom and I became a family.

Now we live in our house together.

We play together and talk together.

We work in our garden together.

Sometimes I wish we had a dad in our family.

But Grandpa takes me to special places.

And we can talk about anything.

And my friend Nicky's dad
is teaching us to play soccer.

I'm glad my mom adopted me.

At bedtime, when we finish telling our adoption story,

she tucks me in and whispers,

"You'll be my little snuggle bunny

forever and always."

And I know she really is the best mom

in the whole wide world!